Playschool Pirates

Written by **Ellie Wharton**   Illustrated by **Amanda Enright**

TOP THAT

Licensed exclusively to Top That Publishing Ltd
Tide Mill Way, Woodbridge, Suffolk, IP12 1AP, UK
www.topthatpublishing.com
Copyright © 2015 Tide Mill Media
All rights reserved
0 2 4 6 8 9 7 5 3 1
Manufactured in China

Written by Ellie Wharton
Illustrated by Amanda Enright

ISBN 978-1-78445-258-2

A catalogue record for this book is available from the British Library

Tomorrow was fancy dress day at school,
but the twins just couldn't agree what to go as.
They had left it right until the very last minute.

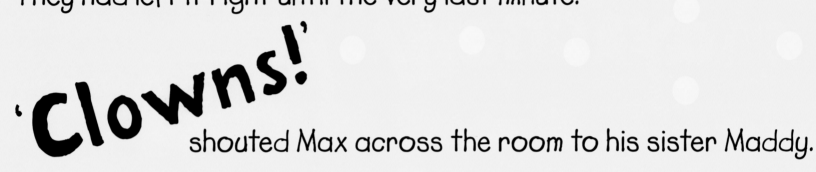

'**Clowns!**'

shouted Max across the room to his sister Maddy.

'**Shhhh** - too silly!'
she whispered.

'**Aliens!**'
he tried again.

'Too scary!' she whispered again.

'Woolly mammoths!' said Max.

'Too ... WOOLLY!' shouted Maddy in despair.

'SHHHHH!' said Max.

Maddy threw a pillow at Max. Max threw one back at Maddy. Soon, a pillow fight began and Max and Maddy got tangled up in a sea of bedclothes.

'I've got it ... PIRATES!' said Max.

'Yes, pirates!' agreed Maddy.

'Pirates **arrrrgggghhh** fun!'

Early the next morning, the twins set about finding their costumes. They crept out of bed and tiptoed around the house.

They borrowed Dad's old telescope and their big brother's bandana.

Maddy found a funny old hat that Mum had once said was fashionable, but which looked very like a pirate hat to Maddy.

They rooted through the dressing-up box to find more pirate-y things to wear. Maddy found an eye-patch and Max found some plastic daggers.

In the playroom, Max found a toy parrot and Maddy found a whale, and they even found an old chair leg for a pirate peg leg!

'What about show-and-tell?' said Max.

'We can fill this empty lunch box full of sweets and pretend it's a treasure chest!' replied Maddy triumphantly.

The twins decorated the box and filled it to the brim with all the sweets from the biscuit cupboard.

When the twins arrived at school
they looked like fearsome pirates!

They made a boat out of a cardboard box and told their friends to walk the plank, which everyone found very amusing.

Then they staged a dagger fight...

and Max wrestled with an inflatable pretend crocodile ...

And Maddy made a crow's nest
at the top of the climbing frame ...

Soon it was time for show-and-tell. The twins opened their treasure chest and everyone gasped.
As they shared out their sweets they soon became the most popular playschool pirates ever!

The teacher was very impressed with how inventive Max and Maddy had been.

'I hereby award the fancy-dress prize to the fabulous Playschool Pirates!' she said, and everyone clapped.

Soon, it was time to go home and Mum was standing at the school gates, ready to collect them.

'Where have all the sweets in the biscuit cupboard gone?' she said, looking at them both. 'You'll lose all your teeth eating that much sugar!'

When Max and Maddy explained that they had shared them out amongst their friends, Mum smiled. Max decided a pirate joke might make her smile even more ...

'Why are pirates great?' he asked.

'Because they

ARGGGGGHHHHH!'

And Mum laughed, proud of her Playschool Pirates.